No Witnesses

No Witnesses

Poems by Paul Monette

Drawings by David Schorr

AVON
PUBLISHERS OF BARD, CAMELOT AND DISCUS BOOKS

NO WITNESSES is an original publication of Avon Books. This work has never before appeared in book form.

AVON BOOKS
A division of
The Hearst Corporation
959 Eighth Avenue
New York, New York 10019

First Avon Printing, March, 1981

AVON TRADEMARK REG. U.S. PAT. OFF. AND IN
OTHER COUNTRIES, MARCA REGISTRADA, HECHO EN
U.S.A.

Printed in the U.S.A.

To Sandy McClatchy and Alfred Corn

Acknowledgments

The author gratefully acknowledges the aid of an
Ingram-Merrill Foundation grant, awarded in
1977–1978 to complete this book.

"Bones and Jewels" received the Coordinating Council
of Literary Magazines award for Best Poem in 1977.

All but one of the poems here assembled has appeared
previously in a magazine. The author is pleased to
acknowledge the support and encouragement of the
edition involved.
Antaeus: "Into the Dark"
Christoper Street: "My Shirts"
American Review: "Degas"
Poetry: "The Wedding Letter"
          "The Safety in Numbers"
Shenandoah: "Bones and Jewels"
              "A Man in Space"
Michigan Quarterly: "The Practice of Arrows"
Southwest Review: "Changing Places"
Massachusetts Review: "No Witnesses"
Orpheus: "Musical Comedy"

Two poems, "Degas" and "Into the Dark," appear in
Daniel Halpern's *Anthology of American Poetry*.

Contents

Into the Dark	1
My Shirts	7
Degas	13
The Wedding Letter	17
Bones and Jewels	27
The Practice of Arrows	37
Changing Places	41
The Safety in Numbers	43
No Witnesses	48
Come Spring	63
A Man in Space	75
Musical Comedy	87

No Witnesses

Into the Dark

To J.D. McC.

I would have run to him, only I was a coward in the presence of such a mob—would have embraced him, but that I did not know how he would receive me. So I did what moral cowardice and false pride suggested was the best thing—walked deliberately up to him, took off my hat, and said, "Dr. Livingstone, I presume?" "Yes," he said, with a kind smile, lifting his cap slightly.

    —Henry Morton Stanley, **How I Found Livingstone**

A spider bite the size of a dinner plate
means, when the thing erupts, that I am strapped
to a tree to scream until I black out. Thus,
God is not my favorite reason why
my shadow knocks and curdles in this damned
chaos. The third day I leave for fever
after two on the trail. The quinine's out—
I think the bearers salt the jungle, since
they prefer to ferment for pain what lies
at hand, the gray grass, bananas, a bark
that tastes like bread. In none of these diseases
do I detect a falling off of the main
madness, covering miles. I double up
with cramps, infected, atilt with vertigo,
and still I manage the next stretch and the next,
annexing nowhere bit by bit to the known
contours. My body's ruined balance buoys me.
I am that sick of the well-controlled.
                           The hills
assert their ups and downs, the violet earth
its pulses and its price. In Zanzibar

the Sultan said: "The gonads grow as fat
as cantaloupes under the sun. A man
has limits. Do consider, along the moon
you mean to map, what can be taken to bed."
As well ask why where the river leads is
worth the losses. I rise above my needs.
The Nile curls a question into Africa
that loosed in the Delta the pharaoh's grip on the sun
and stars, their single aberration. "I
am the world," he dreamed in his gold cloaks, "I
must be the Nile in flood, but what"—as the dream
turns—"what is the gate in the dark which spills
the first water that is my blood?"

                               A woman
has limits too in an hour that sees the Nile
narrowed to a source. Actually, I am
saving myself for a finer bed. A crowd
of girls in New York Harbor sighs at the sight
of my ship. In my head they do. They line the piers
and laugh. I hear them above the mosquitoes
who needle the nets, who eat all night. Who else
but the wanderer can own them, marrying
his inland mysteries at last with hers,
at sea? Is pleasure best following pain
because it comes untroubled by the fright
that leads us *here?* I am of those who hurry,
who would be first or nothing.

                              We're two days
east of Ujiji. Sidh, my scout, ruptured
a column of ants on Monday (careless man)
and must be carried, regularly bathed
in soda, and induced to vomit. War,
I think, forces the jaws on the same schedule,
next to the jungle the test with a victim's
rictus, mere survival. Here, Livingstone

disagrees. He says there is violence
and violence, some of it suffered and some,
the rarer kind, consumed like a weird meat,
a snake's, a crested crane's, once in the desert
a centipede's, oily and sour.
                                        The spice
for sponging off the spider's kiss freezes
my swollen ribs—they go for the heart—and I
order the march resumed. Livingstone shakes
his head. "Sleep the venom out. I will speak
between your dreams, and you will separate
the one from the other on the coast." I nod,
and the night opens.
                                   And yet how queer. At first,
a quiet as fierce as the lost light. Through narrows
awash in ink and pitch, and then a cave
where I neglect to drop a string behind
because I am only going one way. The dark
in certain lights has faces I can see.
Surfacing, I know it has been getting loud
all along. Queerer still, it is purer
than words, taken in change, raw as the dawn
to which it rises up to sing, in which
it dies of exposure. And amnesia is
the shelter at the cave's deserted mouth,
from which I see mirages fume in the dead
distance and, for all of their combustion,
feel the cool of mountain shade. Overnight
the promise of staying lost is broken, much
as you would say the weather broke.
                                                      Livingstone
argues that memory serves to announce
what we can do without. His kit contains
a bar of British soap, a tin of crystal
ginger, shillings, port, tobacco, the end

number of *Great Expectations,* and tea—
kept against surrender, should the desire
arise to fly. "These?" He fingers them. "These
are the other side. There is"—his eyes burn
briefly—"another side. The chain of events,
the river's ruthless indirection, don't
demand tribute except from men"—the fire
gutters —"whom order, the house in the lane, cannot
seduce. Come, disabuse yourself of life
as chosen, as a way of getting better,
it is too fast for such distinctions. See
this ivory ring? A moment ago it was
an elephant."
                    Livingstone puts the Nile
further west, sprung from a mountain spine. The streams
tributary to the Congo finger some
of the same terrain from the east. He dreams a final
fountain playing its two rivers—a lake,
perhaps a falls, unless, for such issue,
a geyser gives the water up. He is
half dead of bites and welts and venom, skin
pied and chipped in places, as if they have
roasted it. With a habit, when he sits
at a map, of shutting his eyes before he looks.

"And so see it afresh. The map projects
the mind's tunnel and gulf. Well, you go down
deep enough, you draw enough approaches
to the map's blank center, do it long enough,
and, Stanley, you can *will* the last of the Nile.
The way to go is by amazement. Cling
to the line of least reason. Let the river
flow uphill, if that will bring you nearer.
The map has the canyons and cracks in the forest.
When *they* disappear, go home."

                                    I will be back,
but Livingstone needs supplies. I will repair
to Dar es Salaam, and he continue south
to Bangweolo, there to rest in a jeweled
city lost on its shores. I will surely
try to come back myself. As a journalist,
of course, I have a certain duty to
a story. Livingstone Alive. In the end,
words are to me what rivers are to him.
Curious, after broken bones, hunger, the stings
and savages, to sweat with horror *now,*
but in my sleep the Nile has drained. We are,
in Livingstone's view, about to finish up
the planet. Then there is just the living
within its fists to do. Where do I start?
I want to get well, I want a woman
and a house in Manhattan, and horses and Irish hounds
on a farm on the Hudson. Livingstone won't attend
to his own future. As a child, I was warned
to turn to stone when a wasp or rattlesnake
was baiting me—then they would go away.
Then they did, now they don't.

                                    Of course I can't
come back, but I will make us kings and get
places for us. "I have swum with crocodiles,"
he says, "in parts of the Nile where nothing kills.
Think of it, Stanley. They come to bathe."
He goes too far. The world is where we live,
never what we think. They swim, yes, and then
they eat. What does Livingstone mean to imply?
I don't follow it. He can *have* the Nile
because I will have *him.* Our names will link,
like lovers. Or brothers. Brothers, if you like.

My Shirts

To Roger

The first was in a window and was silk,
a chemical green. A deep, thin salesman loved
the hang of it, I think, because it lay
by a shoe and an ounce of scent, open
at the throat, and lent a certain air to this
and that. It was, he wanted you to know,
a look that looked ahead, a dream, but not
for everyone. Eighty dollars a week,
his own cut of the pie, wouldn't touch it.

I wore it for an hour and a half. A ride
on a trolley, swinging by a strap. A shot
of Campari in cream, this in a low-life bar,
like cactus liquor on the tongue, the taste
of dread. I kept the glass against my chest,
a rose on a clover ground. And by and by
(but well within the hour), dispensing with
hellos, I fell in bed, the shirt all shucked
like any other skin.
                  The second was,

well, innocent. Tan and wash-and-wear
and went with what you will, none of your swank
and Spanish dancer overtones. Collar
buttons. It was left, as of little worth,
when my friend went to China, where he died.
When he died, Death altered it, but at first
it fit the house I had as well as his,
and so I brought it home. In time it came
to lie in a ball, the day's last apparel, retrieved
at dusk (the stroke of nerves) and shaken out
and slipped on, oh, until I slept.

                         A bad
habit, since it insisted, like the woodsman's
violin in the old story, on taking
the place of things. At the edge of the wood, the bag
of seed, the hatchet and saw fall. The burden
of the tale is local color and German elves.
Sublime, but nothing to do with life. He plays
a piece evocative of autumn light
shaven to edges across the meadow grass,
a light that swipes at the outer leaves but goes
deeper, rifling limb and trunk and root. What
becomes of his cord of oak? Put in its place.
His cut and dried arrangement lives apart.
His violin, see, has bought the night for a song.

One never bewares enough. In the mirror,
with so much to attend to, one doesn't
take the care one ought about the old fool
in old clothes one is turning into, the cheap
effects of the too long loved. What is really
second nature is not the rumpled shirt
thrown about the shoulders of an evening.
No. One seeks the most comfortable way

to carry Death around, to break him in
and thus to wear him out.
                              The third would be,
I swore, my safest yet because I knew
what to watch for—and, too, the risk I ran
that what I would have at the end of the week
was a week's wash. Mostly, a dandy learns
the cost of keeping clean the wrong way round.
His drawers are all in disarray. A shirt
is right for breakfast; then, as lunch comes on,
it seems a shame. Only the droll endure.

Cured of making much of whole cloth, I worked
at random on a patchwork. If I saw
the red was dominant, deliberately
I went to green or brown. No inch of it
led anywhere, lacking the thread. A shirt
without tears, whose surface phenomena
are lovely, like the drift of certain snows,
going on and on until they lead you
to believe they never stop sleeping it off.
And so you hurry home to the fire, the snow
goes to water, and you wake to wonder what
you saw. A shirt, in other words, that seems
guileless. *Is* so, if you stick to surfaces.
Underneath, do not forget, the body
is always sorry for one breach or another,
bareback, prey to gooseflesh.
                              The scraps gave out
in the right sleeve. Remnants I had put by
for years—torn pockets, cuffs the dog brought in
in his teeth, my patches, hems—didn't suffice
or go so far. Far being where the years
had taken *me,* it was a natural

mistake. If time were scraps, I could have plaited
a tent.

      Is this the stuff you want, my love?
My shirts? In a better world, the lovers give
résumés (they have them all typed), a list
of needs, the year that each emerged, and then
the corresponding loss of nerve. In black
and white, all the poop on masks. For instance,
my first arrest involved the theft of a pair
of mesh pajamas. Now I sleep stripped. How
does one explain such reversals? Say this:
that we are sealed to a mirror more and more.
More, we care so for the holding still, we don't
get the joke: its silver and ourselves are
only polish.

      Oh, I know I promised
to fit you with beginning, middle, end.
You would be rags if you went out like *this,*
I know. But wear it now. Tonight is what
we have come for. Tomorrow, when we must
be spiffy once again, something suitable
will turn up, starched and ironed, the one shirt
to which we roll our eyes when we cry "Keep
your *shirt* on" or, in pain, "I lost my *shirt.*"

Well, we will see about that tomorrow.

Degas

To David Schorr

There are so many lies in nature,
a painter talking to painters starts
to lie about the plum and yellow tree
he forks for effect on a storm in purple
paint. The fact is, nothing sticks to
particular colors. A pear in old
grass, shy of the sun's bluff, is
ripe and rotting at once. You mix
a mud green and, green being one
of the lies, a pink and summer gray
appear on the pear, its jaded flesh
as futile to do as smoke.
                                        If the boy
with the wagon is empty to Marseilles,
take the ride. They sometimes favor
fancy detours in view of the secret
sea. The horses at a halt dozed
in a vineyard, I remember, and the boy
fell to his mug of chicory coffee
and milk. Baskets piled in the arbors.

And the perfect blue to break the world on
heaves in sudden sight. You couldn't
actually paint it. Lying, massive,
banked by an African sky and an angry
grapeskin red, a sea like that
will queer your heart. The workers wringing
their kerchiefs love to be sketched, but
they are not mad like the sea to be taken
down.
        I could fuck like a sailor in Cannes.
Madame pumps her baton in a seaside
studio. "Move, little girls," she says,
"like cats. Dance like animals drunk
on their dinners. Simone, what are you?"
"A panther, Madame." "No, today you are
heavy as cows, all of you. Tomorrow
I send you home to your pigs and husbands.
Go to your rooms and practice cats."
Simone, when she models at night, will say:
"You, with your mug of brushes, are
as sour as Madame. You think I am such
a dancer, look at the men who clap at
my recital." I could take her, she's
a beggar for a painter, but I don't. I am
terrible in August.
                    See the sweat on
the jockey's thighs, streaked to his fitted
trousers? Manic from practice. He buffs
his boots, and his manager (here, in the cream
cravat) berates him. See? The chestnut
horse in the middle ground has torn
a muscle. You are not meant to figure
from the picture who has cheated whom.
All the same, it avoids a poster's

thoroughbreds and dark grooms. In my
races, the people bet like the rich,
because money alarms them. About horses
I have no opinion.
      I did a mayor's
wife who posed at a fire from four
to six in a rose salon. Prompt and
uncommonly pale, she took her place
as though for proof if the night came.
Her dilettante hands, a ghost's, I had
to change. Why are we all accused
of motifs? "Another ballerina," my students
write in their Paris journals. "The buyers
buy picnics at the sea. You can always
count on flowers. Degas is stubborn."
When in fact, Degas is probably crazy.
He hates praise. The mayor's lady
is thrilled with the eyes: "I am as pretty
as this," she asks. When she leaves I blot
the hands and do them dead.
        Art is
an artist's father-in-law. They drink
a bit the day the daughter is promised,
at pains to indicate nothing amiss.
They make each other sick. Take it
out on their wives. I don't care what
the Greeks mastered. I am quite sure
of just this, that pent up in jockeys
and dancers the moon tortures the sea.
They pass the delirious night, an addict
couple bloated on green liquor,
relieved of the grief of detail. Apparently
for now, I am the first to know.

The Wedding Letter

There's something you don't know about me yet,
and as it separates the charm of lost
innocence from guilt, it is something *you*
ought to know. When we escaped, when we had
witched the witch and come back to the stone town
and learned to wear shoes and tell the hour right
on the tower clock, the burghers' sharp hearts
were in their throats if we were rolling hoops,
you and I, in the cobbled streets. I think
the city fathers dreamed the witch's tricks
had passed to us like a bad cold. The fools.
Practical men, they accounted us some
insurance against the costlier forms
of chaos. The candyhouse in the woods,
they knew, in part is a house in a child's
head. They were beginning to be a race
much kidnapped from, a country for the old
to quarrel for, and so were glad of us,
who rid the world of the magic able
to barter the soul for a ginger snap.

But something else was eating them. We might
get fickle, splash their wives and eldest sons
with warts. To them, a quest was a bargain
that taught you cheaply not to hope next time
that the deep trees beyond the town grow thin
and clear at the gate of a good story.
A moral with no teeth, having been made
to mythologize the bloody fortune
of those few who left us for the wide world
and stayed away and were, notwithstanding
morals, who we wished to be. We didn't
appear *relieved,* you see. It was a blow
to pedagogy and the harder path
of forks and briars. When you come within
an inch of being battered into cakes
and whipped like cream, you should get religion.

The reason I am writing at such length
is to arm you, Gretel. Tonight, as it's
the last before you marry, is the end
of you and me. But go over to them
out of our sleep and slow roses prepared.
They kill their kind, they die like flies, and love
to sing of it, though why they will not say.
They fruit a tart of what they were and throw
a feast to rid them of themselves, then thrill
to the clean, unhungry past they have just
invented, where they will all go soft. Soon
the swords, the swells of pleasure and the gold,
the brave gray stones pelted at the dragon
lie in their custard hearts. Yet to hear them
tell it, they were born realists and not
young and all wrong. Marry. I don't care. But

there is the matter of my gift, which I
am getting to, my yarn, my thread of seeds
to take us back, *my* way out.
                              What a witch
to happen on. Because her secret wish,
to be a girl, was out of her control,
she ate the lost like vitamins, and sinned
as a child sins, with the mouth, the body
not yet real enough to be a weapon.
Why is a witch, if she is open-mouthed,
omnivorous and rich, all skin and bones?
Because what she eats eats her up. Sorrow,
whose stomach is just the size of its eyes,
stands like a broom in her corner. Not to
be lonely, she might have loved us if we
had had a foreign policy and said:

"Our crazy mother threw us in the woods
because of bread. Now we want to settle
in a kingdom made of sugar. You seem
to need an army, with a house this rare.
Compromise. For protection from the poor
and hungry who locust the land, you would
keep us in cookies. We won't want any
mothering, having had our fill of what
the belly does to love."
                              Murder, of course,
is more your sort of sweet. Fast in a cage
and fattened on taffy, I watched you plot
and execute your first crime of passion.
And death, while it is less diplomatic,
has the advantage of pointed fingers.
The nuns never asked which of us jetted

the gas, assuming *I* saved *you*. And then,
coming home is cushioned by a cliché
as well: all is forgiven, have a slice
of bright berry pie, the past doesn't hurt
unless you let it.
                    But you let it. Why?
You shouldered the oven door like an armed
bandit, and the witch drummed her boots on it,
sizzled and wailed, swore to reform, offered
to cook the moon for you. You were as cool
as a firing squad. And when she was done,
the world stirred in its sleep and threw her off.
Her house, it seemed, was a ring of long lost
children, and it fell like a botched soufflé.
The boys and girls were the mortar and bricks,
and they cracked up like a jigsaw puzzle
of gingerbread men, and off they went, whole.
The gumdrops in their faces were their eyes
again. This done, they had no nightmares left.
"Good girl," the forest called, "not guilty. Make
this girl a general."
                    I can see you,
stealing a look at the clockwork cottage
chiming on your mantel. What do you think
being a wife will change? Our first kisses
smacked of ice cream. Maple and vanilla
hung in the air of our sad nursery.
From the first we had a taste for the strange,
biding its time at the edge of the day's
regular appetites. Call it a set
of defenses for murders yet to come
to light. And tonight, more unspeakable
than our secrets is the telling of them.

I went again. (Did you guess what it was,
that it would be *this* that has made of me
a continuous boy, leading a kite
like the town idiot, on a Sunday
flying it by the church while the town prayed,
slow as a planet?) Back to the break in
the spellbound woods, the tulip trees pulling
the bells of their green hours, the chimney crooked
like a finger in the field, and no sign
that a fat house was thought of there in which
the young would hide from time. Only her great
engine of an oven, cool now under
my fingers, had survived the undone trick
of the building. In its belly, on its ashes,
I would take naps while you went off to court
your dancing master. Whatever we were
left alone to practice, I would put down
to get back to my dream, run to the dear
iron room the witch fired her castle in.
And when, one winter day, I brought in hay
to make a bed and saw how I was home,
there came a knocking on the oven door.
It was she.

        But changed. As young as you
and dressed like a fairy. She had made me
a pastry shaped like a sundial. At each
stroke of an hour, a wave of icing held
a cherry and chopped nuts. A ginger boy
in a chocolate boat was anchored there,
the shadow of his sail telling the time.
The candle in her other hand, she said,
after the pain would leave me free of life
with things to do in a straight town, seeing

they are fatal. *I* would not have to be
a piece of gingerbread. No one would know
from the look of me that I no longer
was involved. And my most secret mission
would be—did you guess?—to follow you.

Poof.

I went up in smoke and woke up a child
forever, far from the rest of you, light
as the paper birds and boxes I hold
high on a string, arrested in the sky.
But I looked like Hansel, and no one knew.

So the past didn't end when you left it,
Gretel, and thus you can't be expected
to be sorry for it. Besides, magic
has other things to be besides a witch.
You weren't that important. That the ice moon
opens again and again is really
no one's fault. It just does. Everyone is
specially scarred by the murder he can't
avoid having on his hands, the killing
by years of one lost child. Go. Go marry
the prince, we want you to. Wear white. The witch,
if anything, is grateful for the push
you gave her into the next mystery.
She speaks of the good luck she plans to rain
on you, who turned her head.

All we ask is

that you get us the ground to bless. Banish
the dwarfs appointed to be your royal
furniture. Make the witch your lady's maid,
and she will sit spinning at the window
singing, filtering like the forest shade

the tribes that travel by, the runaways,
the ambiguous garden retreats of
the prince. And I? A jester, a juggler,
whatever the convention is. We three
will play with power safe in the palace.
Servants will come with trays of fresh candy
and stand as still as tables. If they crack
a smile, they forfeit growing old. Or up,
for that matter.
    Finally, a rumor
of a cure breaks. The line to come inside
snakes with the lame and the colorless out
to the oceans. At our door, where we will love
the best enough to save them, being loved
will stop having its root in what mothers
empty us of because they are starving.

The chance to make us what we were, Gretel.
You can gather the vision you loosed once,
the day you sent the children running home
who had lived in a cake like a coffin
and yet, set free, felt hollow. Like a drug,
sugar scalds if once you take it away.
Every town has one. Out of touch, too
fat, thin in the darks of the eye, shy of
machines.
    Right now, as you read this, the witch
is climbing the tower steps to your room.
Meanwhile, I will guard all the wild candy
stored in the oven. She will lock me in,
she says, to keep me safe. Are you nervous?
You are going to be surprised how much
it is like a mirror, you and she. Yes,

you and she, she says, have always dreamed of
a reunion. Now, as she reaches you,
the wind is filling with flavors, the long
wait ends, and the crumbs gleam in the clearing.
Close as your shadow now. Now she has you
in her charred arms, oh we will be so young.

Bones and Jewels

To Sanford Friedman

Time has simply got to shut up. Or else
I'll beat him senseless, bind his hands, and saucer
his fat bachelor's face like a discus
on the wind. Then let him try to talk of me
as if I had manners and must make do.
Morbid broken boy, to favor those in pain,
turn me twenty-nine without a wrestle
if you can, so long accustomed to tired
women. I have decided to fight you
early—

        because, one, I am on vacation.
Two, I can use my nails, not much given,
in war at least, to honor yet (and yet
I long for forms, for formulas, I mean—
I can't marry now, my darling x. Why,
I can't thread a needle, and my mother
signed me away at birth to z, who is
in oil. My promises, such as they are
are not my own). And three, why I hate you,
you remind me of the men in Maine.

                                    .   Of all
the coasts the sea is heir to, this, this tongue
of Massachusetts, will be taken first—
not, it seems, for several hundred years,
but soon enough. The locals, if they care,
lack the captain's impulse either to sink
with the ship or, like Noah, to pick and choose.
One day, I expect, they will notice how
the high tide seeps among the lilacs (When
did we lose the garden? Wasn't there once
a field as well? And further back, did we,
or am I dreaming, didn't we live high
in the dunes?), and then they will leave the table,
the lobsters cracked and hardly touched, out, down
to the bay to row to Boston.
                            Things to do.
Research before September first the death
of grasses. This far south, when does the brown
come in? Write to Bunny (oh, but lightly).
Ask the Sunday hunter on Ryder downs
why he won't wear red. What is he after?
Stop retrieving shells. The men with buckets,
the tide, the birds won't leave them be. All right,
you leave them be.
                    "Bunny dear, I know you
hate me for a fishwife. I've run away,
where you would lose your temper, have a gin
and lemons, then undertake to reassess
Melville and the whale. The Baptist minister
in town (call him Ishmael) says he won't
dispute the bits of seascape in the Bible.
If they swore that Jonah ate the whale whole,
it is all one to him. Come to Truro,

Bunny (or not! or not!). You are always
in the heart of
>Edna (St. Vicious) Millay."

Fog again. And written down again. Why
bother? Clearly a writer keeps his sad
diary current on ghostly afternoons,
and only then to avert the dark fingers
from the throat. Meteorologically,
assume the worst unless otherwise stated,
as in passages given to paradox,
the notes for a life lived on the loose—
>"Sunny.

From bed"—abrupt, in the New York style—"I watch
Achilles dress. I take my Baudelaire
from under the pillow, play at reading it,
and then write in the flyleaf how he is
something less than Achilles in a tie.
He watches me. He thinks I am doing
a poem, as one does, um, one's knitting
or one's horoscope. We'd kill each other
for a price. Unless we got paid, we wouldn't
trouble to pull a trigger and soil the rug—"

Long since, the bitch with the books and time to burn
has come to the end of America. The heat
she heaps on boys, on warriors and thugs,
belies who is it loves *her* least. She's not
a girl in a story, though the story goes
that she was once so pale, a candle passed
in front of her still lit the room beyond,
no matter how she held it, shook it, blew
and spit at it. Here, pen in hand, she walks

the brink, not in a shawl at the lip of a cliff,
but further than is safe. To tell the truth,
the seas with any drama are confined
to Maine—the undertow, the shoals the shape
of Lincoln's face, and grave after grave troughed
in the open water. Here is, if life is
a place, just the place to write, and no rage
at the edges, no liaisons where the rocks
and water go at it, wasting time.

                                    Three
thirty. The last mail at five.

                            "Dear Wilson,
it has come to the attention of the Friends
of Better Books that poetry, mother
of culture, is practiced now (may I be
blunt?) by riffraff elements. The War has
shaken the temple. Ours is to rally
round the bardic mantle where it is worn
with *style.* Would you, to this end, please inquire
what tone Vincent Millay lately takes. Such
an ear! But there are rumors. Use a ruse.
Go disguised as a weekend guest—"

                                 "Listen,
Bunny Wilson, listen good. The maiden
whore is sorry. Edner M'lay is stuck
for an obligatory scene to close
her broken-hearted book, **The Belle on Board:
A Vassar Girl at Sea.** What do you take
for writer's block? Bring me a fifth of it.
(No, wait. A pint is probably enough,
I have it all written in my head.) And ice.
I can't take medicine neat—"

                            "Who is the best?

Me? I am sick to death of burning bright.
Honestly, Bunny, do I have to be
so Godawfully young? The debutante
champagning in a hooped dress, her daybook
tucked in her reticule. I want to write
The Iliad (at least). And you know what's
funny? I'm old. (I know I don't *look* it.)
I need you here, and I will probably
drive you away. Risk it, rabbit.
                              Your bard."

August 5th. Fog.
                    6th (7th?). Bright out.
At last. Released from a blank tower, no
nearer the moon. Because a woman's body
is a man's clock (due to the tick of it),
she is the one who takes the time. Bathing
is her reward, a long afternoon's soak.
She is given a tub, a shelf of sponge
and unguents; and when she is not in the bath,
she rubs her wrists and temples with a lily
cologne kept cold in the kitchen by her maid.
She buys it by the case. Also bourbon.

Or so I think (I think too much) today,
swimming alone, afloat, tucked in a wave's
hollow jaw. I wish to be occupied
with just my skin. If anyone calls, I'm
being massaged. Unless it is the boy
Time, threatening a scene. It sets him off
to catch me making up and mirroring.
"Hurry," he says, "our car is here. I *won't*
walk in in the middle, like a tailor

given a pair of tickets by a count
who wants his suits perfect. Your gloves are here.
Your furs. Your fan." Oh, we are off, taking
the corners on two wheels. Nothing is said
about my hair.
                    Tuesday. Bunny accepts.
Jesus.
            The beach. Mumbles and Norma waltz
the slopes, careering down the sand, and lean
shoulder to shoulder to hoot at me. Their hats
are whole umbrellas, and they carry striped
canvas sacks as big as awnings. "Tea time!"
Norma cries. At that, as if hurrahing,
Mumbles' hat takes off to sea, going end
over end, a balloon, a kite. Is it
that I can write it down that I will have
forever mother's face caught in the fast
photograph she makes at the loss of a hat?
Halfway down the dune, her hands on her head,
appalled at the wind's perversity. And glad,
because things have a way of staying on
too long. She huffs over *"Baggage!"* and draws
the line, has always drawn it there.
                                    The tea
is tabled on a beached timber, inches
from the ocean. A tart and biscuits, three
painted cups, and wrinkled, mismatched linen.
Mumbles says that, as we're to have a guest
from The City, we must practice eating
normally, one with another again. We've come
to a pass where a bit of pear and crackers
and a book won't do. "Not for *dinner.* We must
be *rational,"* she says, slicing the air
with a spoon. Like old Canute, bellowing "Well?"

over the surf, "What is a little water
to a king?" Our Norma says: "Bunny will think
our meals are like the meals in *Alice,* Ma.
Besides, Bunny is not coming to eat."
We all three titter like spinsters as we pack
our driftwood tea.
               Eleven thirty. Thump.
Someone is bringing a body up the steps
to the porch. The bell. And in comes Bunny, wet
with the night heat: "Christ, it's the lost continent."
He drops his steamer trunk and says, Cockney,
to Mumbles: "Mum, does Edna St. Louis
Missouri live hereabouts?" At midnight
mother produces fish, and now she is
Little Women, radiating gumption
and The Cape Cod Folks. Oh dear.
                   I hound Bunny
with *my* thousand questions about Eng. Lit.
"Like the Eumenides," I tell him.
                    Frown:
"Well, I think you mean the *Sphinx,* don't you?"
                        Hmm.
"Something hungry, then. Fanged. Inquisitive.
And it's got Man's number and eats its young."

One learns to write to write about the years,
one of the Truro sonnets starts. Look at
the second "write." It occupies a place
above the—what?—the fog of sentences
and meaning what is there (when what is there,
if it is true, is far too still to hear).
It doesn't mean, that second "write," *write.* What
am I trying to say? Ah, Bunny knows.

Sunday. Will I marry, he wants to know.
We are throwing shells off Provincetown pier.
I answer lightly, with a line of mine.
No, no, I haven't heard him right. Will I
marry *him?*
        Oh.
                "Oh I can't marry now,
my darling Bunny. Why, I can't thread a
needle, and my mother signed me away
at birth to a mogul. It's out of my hands."
Then, because we are sad, because it is
always better left for another day,
"Give me," I say, "some time. With *two* of us—"
I was going to say the girl's story
stops here, but I don't mean it. It goes on.

Captain Curmudgeon, the man with the cart, halloos,
calling us back, and cuts us short. He's done
the butter-and-egg provisioning for half
Truro, and is the best the village has
in taxicabs. All the way home, Bunny
and I are sailors, keeping the stuff and us
aboard. Some of the time, caught in the ruts
others have wheeled in the way, we click
like a trolley. For the rest, the skipper veers
and blazes a trail, we rattle overland
in fits and starts, and the eggs are on their own.
We disembark at Ryder's field and wait
to watch the captain out of sight, a cloud
of sea birds fanning him off like a sail.

"Would we be the Brownings, Bunny?"
                          Below,

the harbor cups its dream, the going in
and going out only what they are. We
are sea people who do not hold this hill,
this edge, this instant shaped in sand.

       "You mean,
will I take care of you?"

       "Oh no. You must
release me from my father's house."

       "Your father?"
"He is mad. He tells me my paralysis
is fatal. I can do nothing but write."

"Your father's dead. And anyway, you are
a changeling."

    "Literal Bunny. He's not
really my father. More of a boy, really,
but a tyrant. It's Oedipal as hell."

"Will you marry me?"

     "Maybe." (*No* is what
I mean, but there you are.) "In the morning
you go back, and I will mull it over."

And that, as they say in the stories, is that.
Or *would* be, but for the moment on this height,
watching the sun go down. We are foolproof
for a little, though the land is running out
like an hour in a glass.

    Nobody buys
the time in a nice way. It costs the earth.

35

The Practice of Arrows

To Richard Howard

You are apt, on a Chinese dish,
to have a meadow around the rim
and, on the bottom, lotus blooms
and catkins. Rarely, a duck. As it is
not enough that a plate is a plate,
the potter plots his garden. Clay
cuts at first like the scum of autumn
water over which the boatman
passes with his mean and quiet
monk. Ferried to the island side,
to try if the ferns he brushes by
in his dreams grow. His questions bubble
above his head like blown glass.
                                        Once
I am wrong about love, I will
perfect my standard stunt at mirrors
as a dumbshow and go public.
We will eventually play the back
lots of towns so small they haven't
been given television. What

do you think these are? Sequins. And down
on my abdomen I am tattooed—
originally a bear, but still
clearly an animal—which of you
wants to see? The older boys will
pay double to know: what do we do,
who have we done it with?
                                    Do not
knock things from the tables of people
with money, you will jar the grave
of the black sheep captain father out
of Shanghai who, now dead, would stow
a set in a hollow hold for weight.
In the rain his wicker chests upturned
and boomeranged under the deck.
Ah wait till you see, he writes, *your bolt
of peacock silk. Porcelain too,
if the wind permits. Beneath me here
it shakes like Satan's chains the day
he went to pieces.* Do not take
coffee at all if you can't compose
your hands. Say it's an ulcer.
                                    Could
you kill, you could appraise the need
not to. You are accessory
to murder each way you relish
the paralysis of land that lacks
moving targets. Don't, the master
glazer cautions, introduce ducks
much before the ivy riots
the bank and various flowers are out
as deep as enamel, as if from sheer
hunger they are anchored in the lake,
treading on an industry of weeds.

Apprentice yourself to him and he
is who you are.
                    Just at the last,
the master sits fixed on a dwarf tree's
one red leaf, planted (it is said)
by a martyr who wept the seed
(or bled it, wounded in a hunt,
mistaken for a bear). You try
an arrow shot at the island hill
that uses up its thrust in flight
and lights like a dragonfly. Out
comes the finger of the monk. Because
it is ammunition, because
it has come in his dream, he comes
to include it.
                    As to who to be,
Rilke's letters are numbered one
to ten like symphonies. In the eighth,
in Sweden in August, he says: be sad,
dragons are half of them princesses,
"only waiting to see us once
beautiful and brave." The boy became
the boy he wrote the letter to.

A dish acquires a code of old
surfaces, whatever its
conventions. This year goes, and this,
and this is the truth as the truth
goes, according to what's intact.
Start with a cup of weapons. Sit
so you squat like a duck, they won't
presume on a man in prayer. Well?
Shoot what you have to shoot.
                    Burn this.

Changing Places

To Nick

The last tenant has left a dead address.
Inoperable, the ill-kept agent says
(in confidence, she says), and systematized
in a terminal home. I picture the man,
apprised of his roaring blood and out of luck,
when he left. Having ordered his closets and not
his life (come to take it over, I am
simple with contempt), he stands
unpacked, obituary copy. Since
I clean him out for nothing, I am heir.
I trash his interiors. Prints go to the dump,
the books in cellar boxes, that he might
get better in the end and send a cab
to take them. I stretch my deathbed grin
in his mirror and spoons. He needs a rest, yes,
his book of appointments proves it. Anyone would.
But I get to a point (a Monday, cool,
the mail late), happening on a list tacked to
a cupboard, I am sick of finding him.
The city has gone into shock, and over its bad

nerves the dead bring cancer. A mover hoists
into his idled truck the movables
of some release. Live light, I like to think,
and live without the mortgage on time. Oh but
Doctor, I have noted a string of pain
below my heart, a whole ball of it, and
when I run away it worms across
my blood. I wouldn't mention it except
a small fatigue has lately overcome
the man before me. Isn't it odd (or is it
just in their heads) the citizens of my
apartment go to flush the enemy
once they settle. I'm all right, Nick, how
are you? "Thank heaven," says Thoreau, "here is
not all the world." He isn't praying: heaven
isn't either. Short of building, you get
germs. I stay with a specter so like mine
I give it room. This envelope, for instance:
his or my own? The carrier doesn't care.

The Safety in Numbers

To Roger, one autumn night.

The dead don't go to college. If they did,
they would major in life. They take the risk
of coming back, I know, as a matter of course.
For instance, Halloween. They go disguised
as children, knocking, avaricious, dead
of the usual (loss of heart), out to pinpoint
what went wrong. I would have said, before
we were entangled, that the dead *possessed*
the children, but they steer clear of purists.
Their real target is a man making (love
is the typical cause) a compromise.
The leaves are down. The scavengers, long since
the architects of spring, no longer deck
the nests, are flown, and eat October up
orchard by orchard, lying low at last
like widows in the south. Wintering is,
as practiced by birds and the well-to-do,
an instinct for evasion. Northern men,
who walk powdered with frost (and frost is just
the beginning), must make deals. "Oh love," they say,

"curl up with me, the wind will leave us be
once we are twined. Dress if you must and go,
but if the weather has it in for us,
you won't make it home."

How the dead *study*
such transactions. They sit at their marble,
monumental desks and read statistics,
charting what are the ways, besides a box
and a hole, of cutting loose. Curing the year's
ruin was, in their day, the work the best
took on. Investing in fuel and aspirin.
Making a killing on the common cold.
They never prized winter as lovers do,
as camouflage, when the weather is blamed
for the psychic scars, for grief, regret, at night
for the dread of climbing stairs. We say, to say
something, "Out there, things have frozen solid.
When will the whistle in the wind end? Feel:
my hands are ice."

We mean to divert the gods'
attention, make them think the air is smoked
with our diseases every time we breathe.
The black branches spider against the dire
white sky, the nerves removed, a fall of snow
predicted. We admire the absolute
in anything. The more precipitous
the drop to zero, the more perverse the wind,
the deeper does it drive us into secrets.
Too late the dead have caught the gods staring,
hammers high, into their beds, hungry to ask
(at the first coo of pleasure) what's so funny.

"Take one dead man," said Emily Dickinson,
who lived exclusively in mid-November,

"in *his* eyes flock and freeze the prisoned birds
who—undecided—linger like the guest
who can't, because she hasn't caught the drift,
depart the party yet—certain to err
if she *guesses* of whom to take her leave.
So on she waits, until only the two,
the Host and she, are left. 'You must, my dear,
remove your mask,' she says. He says, sending
the bolts home, 'But I did.' "
                              In Halloween
a spook finds a vehicle one night long
with which to cruise among the data. Once
the Celtic priests decreed the last of October
the end of the year (and cut it in Celtic
all over Wales) and made it the rule of the day
that the restless dead resume for a little
this cupboard of blood and bones, to scatter abroad
like bats and hags on brooms and wolves, to research
the reason why, why in the world we sleep
alone. Then the virgin birth, the star type
of love in a single bed, reorganized
the calendar along religious lines,
reserving to the saints a haunted night
of their own. They touch down in a tractored field
brought to its knees by fall. Now they are whole,
they feel no physics still equating them
to earth. They sigh. It is the saints' relief,
in fact, that blows these trees of ours to bits.

Come on. The brainless riders have no time
for us. They have their hands full—the pumpkin
that was their head, the stallion's flying mane—
they are holding on for dear life. The dead

46

have got to pass exams to graduate
and so commit the men to memory
they find in love. We are much better off
outside, howling like skeletons. Let them, for love's
unevenness, for time's tired sake, think
we are as wronged as they. Even in jest
we may see why the world is preferred. Why
do you jump? Howl back. Or get behind me.
Let be if a nightmare springs up in the path.
"Boo," if it's human, will chase it away.

No Witnesses

To Gertrude Macy

> *The real American type can never be a ballet dancer.*
> —Isadora Duncan

Nice, 1927

Kiss it. Kiss it oh oh
                  stop I'm sore
                           mm,
we're both raw in the wrong place, my darling,
to go so far again so soon. Lie back
and let that tiger sleep. Here are your black
cigarettes. Now watch: in motion there is
more of me. One of my theories is:
when any of my centers smarts—head, heart,
belly, sex—the dance I dance I dance *there,*
around the sting My Life is throbbing with
then
     and then, in the eye of The Dance, the pain
sees, and what it sees is Beauty, stopped dead
in its death rush, smiling over its bare shoulder,
its breath drawn. This that I'm doing here is
Sex, since an ache is groping deep in me.
It is all love's fault, but dearest, only
a girl would say it hurts.

The whiskey? Why,
there in the bar. No, *there*. Let me get it,
you go back to bed. I must be your first
taste of this hotel. The territory
baffles you. Insist on The Negresco,
Cocteau said, because there is always ice
and the ice is blue, from the lakes of the lower Alps,
it clears the lungs. And so discreet, he said,
they don't send a bill. I have kept this suite
for weeks, though I don't have a sou. Money,
I find, is relative. Like youth.

                         And they say
Isadora is good business. The tears
in the lobby, the telegrams. A Dutch banker,
told of my *passion* for raspberries, empties
a penthouse and carpets the floor with them,
three inches deep. He begs me to dance there
and beat out a wine to cloud his head. These
circuses have always dogged me. One day
they will learn I don't do cures and whore's work.
But the room, the rumor goes, is booked ahead
and much requested. Though it is clean, it draws
my bad admirers still. They want stray fruit,
the unspied thing that rolls like a pearl under
a bed and smells of me.

                         For thirty years
I've been as young as you. It doesn't work
but it feels good, and it passes the time,
like this hotel. Watch:

                         my arm in the air
is the arc of an egg, always in flight
from me. It seemed, the day I did it first,
the wand I would own to be born from, bodied
as a wave, as a wing

                     and still my arm.

I don't try to hide it. Loving all night
and like a fire are side effects of The Dance.
The Greeks, my brother Raymond says, did not
distinguish love and life, but of course he means
Greek *men*. A Greek woman tampered with neither,
with nothing but her sons, in whom the slow
loss of a girl's almonds and tentative feet
proved false what she and the earth believed, that they
could make stand still their most rushed runners, who are
giant with change, afoot before they know
where it is safe.

        For my Greek dances, I pass
across the tidal line from men to women.
Breath in, shoulders frozen, it is all done
at the belly, where the body starts like a car.
Look, since I can't explain. First, a warrior
waving a saber, his city sacked. This blade's
whip whip whip is his own war, and it goes
like lightning until

        he doesn't know why
he can't just stop. He's tired. His poor left ear
is probably severed, and there is something sad
he can hear for the first time. Death, but a Death
sick of dying. He cocks his head. In the pause
a nobody runs him through

        ah

        he buckles,
becoming his wife in labor, and the pain
can't touch her, though it turns her inside out.

To be both, I bleed. Blood is the breakthrough
down in the dizzied heart. You see? You don't,
your animal proves it. Hot and out prowling,
with a shiver like a tuning fork. A man
would make a lunatic woman—he lacks

the inner mirror and the wit to kill
the wish to be a man. The reverse depends.
Oh presently I will kiss it up and down
and then ease it in, but first I have to
talk over the boy you remind' me of, all right?
I will lie next to you like this. You play.

When I was young (though no one is—it is
a sentimental lapse of the almost old),
I met everyone, but only once. Faster
than I, Isadora stripped Europe, undid
its fussy buttons, and replaced its priests
with men aroused by the sea and the night's hard
music. I followed the rumor of *that* Isadora
wherever it went, and was she, and so
was not. Not a riddle: Isadora
is not the dancer dancing, as a dream
is not an ascent, though the lookout abounds
with the lot of your life's brief houses and the fall
is long. On tour, I anchored by accident,
falling in with kings and the like, and off
on the next train.
                    I thought Doctor Freud was
the man who did the mending—it would take
a tailor to look so cursed by the body's reach,
its straining at seams. You felt he was his best
in a closet or, better, a double-doored armoire,
the costumes hung, the disguises never worn.
"It's this tunic," I said. "Vienna, I think,
is past time for a new idea. Hems
up."

        "As you wish." He smiled, or felt he did,
"But I come empty-handed. And Vienna,
I fear, is not recovered from the last
breaking of ground. Snuff?"

                    Unscrewing the head
of his cane, he held it steady and snapped the lid.
He was the opposite of me. We shied
like an athlete caught in a room with a scholar,
then found we had in common my beloved
ancient Greeks, who were always both, and so
spoke of the climate that favors cities, gods,
and the cutting of stone. My dressing room was just
an affair of screens, makeshift, no tea, no beer.
But as there was fruit and this was Freud, I
peeled and bit a banana. He declined,
fussing instead with his cigar. We were
a self-contained erotic joke, because
the great are furious with the great, never
admitting one another right away,
as chiefs make peace first with squid at dinner
and native shows. When there are no witnesses,
the *very* great populate Athens, some such
exercise of shape outside the white hotel
of having learned the truth.

                    Hey. You wake up.
Come on, come back to Isadora. Don't
underestimate the worth of these
indiscretions—the *cash* worth, my darling.
Or, after all these days naked with me,
do you still not see what people will do
to get at an untold story?

                    Nothing happened
between Freud and me, it is the boy involved
who will amaze you. I agreed to go,
for a week, to a country house where a young man
had been driven mad, the doctor said, by art.
"Artists *are*," I thought, but went anyway,
because the manias money permits are sad
and are chosen over The Dance. Big money

became my enemy the day my feet
left the ground. Any opportunity
to spy it green is a chance to kill it.
I walk through a castle like an earthquake,
though I smile a good deal. I went with Freud
to meet the competition.
                         The studio faced
due west, its floor tiles warmed from underneath
by water pipes. A pianist. A cellist.
A sullen girl from La Scala who doubled
at sets and make-up. And the boy, today
Narcissus bent at the water (here, the glaze
on the blue floor), wearing thin, insensible
of the earth aired and fired to fashion this China
river, missing the joke, as if the Alps
breathing down his white neck didn't prove it
a fallacy that nature is as fine
in its mirroring, as beautiful as we.

"What does he stare at?"
                         "Why, himself."
"Oh that," Freud scoffed. "The self is just a way
of asking the question again. What does he *see?*"

"Nothing like a lake, if that's what you mean. Most
of the hard edges go. Narcissus saw no
water, saw no self even. His beloved
is what he would *say* he saw."
                                "Good. But where
do they learn the word? They are cruelly polite,
for the most part, tend as a group not to
have left the grounds, and their mothers are dead.
What perfects the image they have of The Other
with whom they confuse The Self?"

                              The question,
since he spun on his cane and let it hang,
was meant rhetorically. With more of a hat,
you know, and a feel for sex as a little toy,
he would have trotted just like Chaplin. Jaunty.
(Take special note of this. Someday they will
memorialize Freud too solemnly, always
sitting down, like Lincoln. The accuracy
of biography varies inversely with
the piety.) I wasn't cowed a bit
by questions (he left them behind all the time),
and the answer is this,
                        that The Other is
The Self *danced*. (In the passive voice. We speak
of a danced dance. The verb doubles back with practice,
like the body.) An artificed Self, living
as slowly as a rock. When Raymond and I
slept in the Parthenon, I woke in the dark
and, propping myself against a column, cried
when I felt it warm between my shoulders.
As slowly as that.
                    But I had been engaged
to teach the boy to dance. Plainly I was
misinformed. Expecting an idiot
weeping expensively, dressed like Byron,
I wasn't myself and wasn't prepared for such
gesture and engagement, the holding on to forms
by intuition. He danced with none of the mean
economies, none of the cut flowers
of the second-rate.
                    "Do you do the death scene?"
I asked, seeing he was past compliments
and the mummery of praise. (Dancers die of it
early on, and when they don't, they die of

their rioting muscles. That is why the Greeks
died young, to keep the Elysian meadows
quick.)

   "No." He came to his feet. "There was no *scene*
to speak of. The water hypnotized him so,
he fell in with a little plop, without
a struggle, swallowed like a toffee. Myths
for me reduce to the final pause before
the sky goes yellow and the clocks break down.
I shave away at that moment, then I
blow it up large, full face. What do *you* do?"

"Well"—imagine how I liked him—"I
am more concerned with the hero's solitude
after the thunder is done. Myth is a place
without an audience."

   "Oh that," he said,
but smiling. "The plain without borders or trees,
and the bent figure there: this has not happened
to anyone else, and no one else is lost
to tell him what it is. Teach me that, yes,
because I don't believe in it. I think
the lightest feet freeze when the customers
withdraw. Myth is theater, though Isadora
combines the two, in the way that nature does.
There isn't much time. Train me."

   "No, we will
collaborate. Which of the Greeks' fictions
has two principal roles?"

   "Orpheus."

   "Fine.
The tunnel out of hell. Get some clothes on."

I forgot to tell you, he was naked,

and as heavy as you are there, at the root,
half the time cocked in a full salute. Oh wait,
I'm almost done, don't finger me, not yet—
I'll sit over here on the steamer trunk
so as not to tempt you. Well, to tempt you
more. No it's all my fault, I touched you first.

So. We practiced steps in a statued garden
hard by an Alpine meadow steeply set
on a mountainside, where a low wall (was it
perhaps a stream?) cut the two greens apart,
the two kinds of flowers. The boy and I
did leaps and held very still and stretched flat
in a bed of herbs, and Freud sat on the edge
of a pedestal taking notes, right under a stone
statue of Love with her hands in her hair.
He never spoke, but we were always three,
a company of dancers and the resident
critic.
        In two days we outgrew the work
of exercise and plain technique, content
to do some of it blind if we could start
(and wanting to avoid thinking it out
in advance, or else why dance the thing at all?).
For the hell's path, we chose the walk along
the broken wall. There was a stream as well,
parallel, which the wall followed, or both
a long time past began by following
the walk. The human urge comes first.
                              We came
down the garden that morning like a wind
heavy with the next season. We went in a line,
the boy ahead, then I, then Freud. The wall
had shed stones in the path and kept us slow.

Later, at intervals known only to him,
the boy turned round. Trying it angry or sad
or seized with doubt. I would fall back. Curtain.
And so we made our way, playing the scene,
to the wall's end, where the water ran under
a hill. All meadow here. I don't know where
the garden left off. Or the doctor. Freud
had been at my back, puffing, but he couldn't
keep up, it seemed, or had a stone in his shoe.

Again we took our parts. This time the boy
turned *laughing,* and I saw, as I fell,
what they do to joy in a myth. Orpheus
was *tricked.* At hell's lips, the sun clapped its hands
to see him home again, and he forgot,
whirling to his love and savage song, that the sun
was not the judge here. She was a heart's beat
behind, a foot from the light. He brought his hands
to his eyes, hoping the underworld had not
noticed, but she was already gone. Spinning
with love's bad luck, I did a hell's fall, drawn
back to my demon master, lost by a cursed
singer. The boy snapped.

                    "Bravo," I thought. Dazed,
in a trance, he stopped, changing into the blank man
who just survives, who happens to. From where
I lay at his feet, I felt him turn to stone
and thought, "He's right. There is nothing to dance
in the end."

                    "You win," I said. He stood his ground,
and I began to stroke his leg, his knee,
when the bushes parted like a curtain
and Freud stepped out.

                    "Where have *you* been?" I asked,
making a game of it because I *knew*
he had watched us perform from the front row,
and I didn't care. We were wonderful,
after all. I am used to good notices.

"He has lost his senses," he diagnosed,
    tapping the temples.
                    It was him against me.
"Oh no you don't," I said, "he has *found* them."
I came to my feet. Near us three, I could see
the wall and the water's course take hold again.
Far off, the boy's house stood on the valley
like a fortified town. The world was curious
but real. And yet I saw it was all true,
the boy was prisoned in his own head, numb
at every door.
                    "It wears off in a few days.
Typically the eyes recover first,
then the ears, et cetera. But the limbs
stay rubbery for weeks. Take the left arm."

We led him home. His bed had been prepared
(All, all of this had been foreseen), a car
ordered for me. I couldn't touch the plans
because they were not The Dance. I was through,
and the nurses sprang to the boy's side. Freud feels
that life is such an emergency, it goes
without a clue unless it's microscoped,
in quarantine. I was not consulted,
but let that alone. *I* feel the opposite:
examined, life gets deadly. Do we need
this boy? The years are a mess without Art,

that I knew, but that for the pure they are
the same mess *with* had been held from me. Still
I flee it. There is work to do. Time will
have to be replaced more utterly
by Art than being young allowed. When I
pulled away, Freud stepped on the running board.
"Hems up," he said, as if to spur me on,
and then was gone.
                           The end.
                                         Now, kiss me. More.
What? No, I never see anyone twice,
I told you. The second time can't be danced.
Maybe the boy came to his poor senses
and went to law school. Or else he cracked up
diving deep in his floor. These things will hinge
on whether you *want* the boy to get well.
I keep my mysteries open-ended,
sometimes for the sake of art, sometimes for the day
when someone seems so much like someone else,
I tell it again to see if it's true.
                                         Come,
what can the body do but go on, when
the best of us are eaten from within?
After the first time, you don't ever stop
being in hell, but you still climb. Our own
days in the flesh shuttle us there and back.
And the heart really breaks at a bad ending,
but it leaves no witnesses. It guns them
in cold blood.
                           Now kiss me. The truth is,
we doctor the ancient dances every time
we go to bed, or they drive us mad. You see why.

Come Spring

I told him he must beware of finding and booking it, lest life should have nothing more to show him. He said, "What you seek in vain for, half your life, one day you come full upon, all the family at dinner. You seek it like a dream, and as soon as you find it you become its prey."
—Emerson, *Thoreau*

I

It would make a man pencil-shy, almost,
to hear Thoreau's hard breathing at the end
when, like a miner, he retreated to
the wet house of his winter lungs. The air
was radared, particled with graphite dust
thrown off in fashioning the tool that can't
cut wood or core holes in a post. We write
in ink if we have something good to say,
but if the family trade is pencils, then
one works with one's resources. And Thoreau
was a wizard in the business. Also
like a miner he had picked the outer
shell, to go to the hard part, the long night
seeded after the summer green. Who did
not die in the old days of some bad air?

II

You may know this: the book wasn't written
out there but after, at a desk in town.
Well? Is Walden then a fiction? You know,
what marks us in this inquiry is not
who knows the most. We will agree to share
the facts. But look: like God, the myth is most
unequally divided. And, writers
not included, it makes people happy
to smell a rat. He went so far, it seems,
as to year a calendar for his notes
on Maine, done in the present tense but not
until he landed home. The most of you,
crestfallen here, should go read Stephen Crane.
But if you see him telling lies like you,
for time, arranging to hold on, the past
possessed at last as almanac, listen:
Thoreau's desk is a parlor model. Not
wide as a meadow. The writing surface
is the size of a keyboard. For an aunt
built like a bird, for invitations to
a parish supper. Feel how narrow lies
the ground of his undoing of the earth.

III

Who no longer wander Walden: otter,
woodcock, the reckless loons. But wait: one could
go on like this all day, and catalogue
mammals and birds, the endangered species,
until the list was respectable, a
Museum of Natural History,
like, but in the head. The pond is deeper
than it is extinct. Thoreau, Concord's best
surveyor, plumbed it to a hundred feet,
a hundred four, but the point is it was
bottomless before that. Canada geese
fly at thirty-two feet. Depth divided
by height comes to three and a fraction. Prove:
using a like method: a house is what we
say it is. A culture can't, until
it codifies pi and zero and the types
of fire, have parabolas. It dreads
what else its measurements are of. It must
invent the figure 3 to say in feet
how far I go in a footfall. From there
to the bullet that wipes clean on impact,
changes into a pip, sprouts a lily
that, sniffed, inhibits the will to weep for
nine generations, is just a matter
of time. Do not measure your going much.
Thoreau, who put the end of the world on
the map, hated the short cut he wore to
the water. Multiply the distance lost
by the time saved. This gives you the number
of vanished animals. Fretting dodoes,
mustang, stripe-skin tigers. If you can't put
two and two together, you must throw up

a house by guesswork and by paradox.
His sermons and economies obtain:
to add, you must subtract; to stay, get lost.
Thoreau is the most gone. None of his books
makes much of where. Away. Some few hide out
with him. Turtles, adream in a dome. Frogs.

IV

Thoreau's aunt, a scented hanky patting
her neck as if she and not her nephew
might argue with the air and turn sky blue
in a strangle, visits after a fashion.
Not known to love bodies of water much.
She sends wishes from the foot of the stairs,
in case she should catch it. An apple bloom
sachet fairied among her laces, since
she is sure these diseases of the lung
have death's odor, like dirty hair. "Henry?"
Asked of the upstairs hall. "Tell me, have you
made your peace with Him?" They are unmarried,
the two of them. "My darling Aunt Emma,
I didn't know we'd quarreled, He and I."

V

We *would* say sing if spring would come and stay,
we would sing and say *nothing* if it came.
It comes wincing. In March we crack in two
with the waiting, gasping up in our rooms
while the frailer thing that we are about
to become, paying a call below, wears
the first thought of apples in her hair. Spring
comes like a new winter starting. Taken
together, they meet in a bad week, week
and a half of rain. Days like killers pull
the year through, the fruit out. If I acquire
waterfront property, an acre so
sited that its fingers lie in Walden,
I probably throw up a barn. To fetch
the creatures from the air, corn and millet.
Hay for the random cow. As if the book
won't sell without a lot of autumn. Nice
people are kind in the same way, russet,
ripe, tidying up. Intuiting he
would never make provision for the night,
she frauded his name on a dotted line
and made Thoreau a man of property.
Against his will she cleared him a wind-cleaned
high site, a grave like a bedroom window.

VI

Some witness, huh? The mid-April, eighteen
seventy-five morning papers feature
Concord's two kinds of old women. The rich,
bred hard to show how housed the battled town
had grown to be, the long-landed ladies
who, it fell out, owned the fields their fathers'
literary reasons won for them once
to make their gardens of, their houses on.
And the unamused, whose husbands love them
and live by this: the one life given to
water is given too to ice and air
and so moves in two ways, by running off
and by changing its mind. This aunt we have
devised, this poodle Unitarian,
doesn't know which she is. A tea-pourer
at worst: the President (Grant?) himself is
making remarks and must be fatted. Or
a nuisance, bannering right in the square:
"Who was so freed at Concord, gentlemen?"
Damn all centennials and dumb speeches.

VII

Well, let her be neither. Let her unearth
in her attic Henry's map of Walden
crayoned on a live leaf, long gone to Braille.
Let her go. Out of town, spring has taken
small chances and does not parade. Where she
comes from, water is measured by what it
waters, by cups and quarts. But hey, will you
look at this country coming back awake,
rivering, brooked, the slow and leafing trees
made simple in the blur on Walden. So
one comes here to be young, she thinks. Pretty,
really, but so (oh) relentless, starting
afresh because the year forces it to.
House her out of season then. Time allows
no monument, her nephew knew, but time.
It won't set a stone on a stone. Keep this
from her, who says she is such a lady.
Train on her heart some lie, of a Walden
frozen just this side of May, with its crack
perfume and light diamonds. Tactfully,
she will suppose it is only water,
only more so. Not the sea, but something
of the sea's sleep at bottom. A day's sail
from her own door, and deep, like a nice book.

VIII

It comes. Year after year you cough and croak
and leave no tracks, the last of the breed,
winter having won. You rattle your death
at April, and fleetly, in ones and twos,
the rare animals pad on their last legs
at your blue feet and knit their nests. They want
changes made. 1. You are king. 2. Save them.
"Don't ask me," you say. "My house is a book
that leaks. It was a zoo last summer. Once
it had the look of being true. Now this."
And for what? You wake up warm one morning
and shut up. You can't have for the whole year
the dry and level voice to call Walden
the earth at a grown man's door. The thing is,
who is *not* Thoreau May first? Thoreau, who
was Thoreau all the time, died too damn soon
for us to have it from him straight how spring
is mountained in us like a thing being
written down because it didn't happen
but, once written down, does. I admit to
most of the common sorrows. And to hours
penciling rooms on the paper I meant
to live by words. I have caught a shiver
that comes and goes. The sun sings it to sleep.
The difference between me and him is
I am afraid to speak of it for fear
that spring willfully sends out false alarms.
It trees and leaves inchmeal, as if it knows.

IX

Crazily, the loss that muddies the way
to Walden is the sleep this startled earth
surrenders. The natural approaches
of just a week ago have softened, all
inexact, and we seek Thoreau instead
of us. Because there is no chronicle
of *us* in which the heart is home. After
he died of a cheap joke, we came here, galled
not to be singled out to carry on
the written work. And raw, the first full-blown
Americans, driven from house to house
the moment something rots. The year hires us
as detectives just to keep us busy.
There are things it wants us to overlook.
It plants a clue or two about Thoreau,
letting it out that he's fuzzy and safe.
Him? He has hunkered down to watch us both
in a near thicket, that dangerous, that
in love with those who hate spring. So we have
failed to find him, but what that means is this:
we will be harder next year, and so on.
Why do I say *we?* *You,* for all I know,
are angling for a post way off in spring's
torn country. You have started to wheedle,
I know, and the aunt was your idea
as much as mine that led us into spies
and sources. The morning star like a pulse
beats in the dim sky, and our lightless airs
have put up shop. The sun is in on this.

A Man in Space

To Walter McCloskey

*Some changes in the design were made as the work went on, in compliance with
real or fancied necessities of convenience for construction . . . so that the actual
building at present lacks, perhaps, the unity of the original design without
attaining a new unity of its own. I am past caring.*
—Henry Hobson Richardson

New Year's Eve, 1876

A hundred and three and a sixth. Feet. In meters
it is neater, but I trade in local
currency. You must be Vanderbilt. I'm
Richardson. I saw you here, sizing up
how high we've gone in Boston. "To the sky,"
as the masons must have sung at Chartres,
sending each other up, taking their turns
high in the towers, hexed by those dragons
and lean saints no one can see from the ground.

The snow has let up. You are good enough
to come at all on such a night, but come,
sit with me on the steps a minute first,
before we go in. I'll just spread this fur,
you don't mind. The men keep a stove coaled here,
out front, to toast the night policeman's feet—
to keep him on his toes, I think. Or if
the law falls asleep, then let it at least
bed down by *my* bloody church and *scarecrow*
the vandals. By day the men warm up at it.

I'll tell you a secret. I've made a name
being a father to my men for sheer
minutiae. An iron-belly flame
burns on site for one man's comfort: mine. (Yours
as well tonight, Commodore. I'm a host
before I'm an architect. The best are.
Why build except to bring the world inside?)
I run from fire to fire all winter long.
In fact, I even eat like a dam bear
as winter comes, as if my blood called out
for the thick of a long coat. I root at this spot
when the project needs me, my hands to the heat
as if to beg it to work. Deep winter
about murders me. (The second reason
to room the measureless abyss is old:
throw the cold off.)
                        But let me offer you
some wherewithal. You'll like this chambered box—
apothecaries were itinerant
in the dark ages between the wheel and the first
railroad. A small town's stranded houses stand
about the phantom ancient hearth. Its priests
and doctors can't leave well enough alone—
they get itchy on a sunny day and start
banning games and dancing. Everyone stops
for his own good, but when the medicine man
carriages in, his medicine chest in hand,
they crowd his all-day show. His opened box
is more than pills and powders. In small ways
he's the killer of time and pain. The blur
and early spasm, come from living nowhere,
need to be deadened. And a specialist
in storms of the skin and hair will render numb

some neighboring fear. All in a portable shop,
presto.
            You see I've had it fitted out
for riding in Boston, where the cabs
are infamous for moving in circles.
Bourbon, brandy, and pipes—the staple goods
in ravished cultures. Louisiana,
my native land, is less American
than Byzantine. We're bred to think decline
beautiful, slow, and comical, more
like a marriage than a disease. A tragedy
cannot be gone to like a party, so
no one gives them. Content to live on edge,
we never buy from medicine men unless
we're out of what to start the evening with.
Our homes embody principle number three:
build with every penny. Even go broke
if you must. The alternative is mean,
a coffinful of space.
            Nothing at all?
I would not be sober for Richardson's
New Year's sermon, but suit yourself. I know,
we should get down to business. Talk is cheap,
and we have money to burn if I have read
your letter right. You want a monument.
No restrictions. Whatever it should cost,
wherever I put it, no matter if
it looks like a slaughterhouse—*it* gets built,
I get paid.
            You see why I need a drink.
Out of the blue, the man who could afford
the Taj Mahal midases me. The fee
to be five times my previous high or half

77

a million, whichever is more. Easy.
Anything with a million in it is more.
"Answer expected on the thirty-first,
when client will be in Boston for the night,
unless holiday gets in his way, or yours."

Mine? We are sitting on the steps of mine.
Trinity Church, when it is done, will be
the Boston Vatican. We consecrate
six weeks from now, and so tonight it is
no more holy than a factory. Doubtless
God has gone in to inspect, but he is not
in residence till February ninth.
In the meantime, *I* am the head of the house—
just as soon as I am warm, we'll go in
and see if I am there, throned in my own
stone skin, silent as the banker's banker
leaving the bank last, his squint eyes lifted
to a dome of his own, where once he was so small

There's another law lurking in all that—
a man has houses other than the rooms
where he sets up a lady with a staff
of worn out Irishmen. His offices,
his club, his railway car are figures for
a castle he pieces together—first
in his head, looming, then on a stretch of shore
when the money's all in.
                              Do you know what
winter is best at? Rules. It says the same
dumb thing in every tree, and when it has
our attention, it rattles off the unities
its snows unclothe. The green particulars
are what our windows face, our own rooms set

so that we seem to stand among birches
when we part the curtains—the winter knows
how like a tree our dreams are cut. And yet
the laws that are still left at Christmas speak
like men who work and feed and, questioned why,
say that is what men do. The wind ticks off
the regulations, blown from the land of forms.
It lays us flat who live in the woods. The trick's
to brace your feet and fix in the glacial air
a house of fire.

        You like that, I can see.
You think: a lighthouse, at the very least,
lashed to an island, mortared in a storm
and rocked by sea water, light like a cry
knifing through. Give it up. The best places
are taken, the whole East coast all beaconed
up and down like the Milky Way.

               Patience.
Building buildings is slow. My ancestors are
the priests of the Romanesque, their rough sketches
of steep space, just the act of making seen
as a tonic for the unconstructed heart.
Back then it took two wars, a plague, a king
who rode in blood and five full revisions
of God's right to the real estate to rafter
a finished church, perhaps a hundred years.
The word is made flesh in its own good time.
The architect there, a monk conditioned to wait,
was happy if half a tower, an arch,
or only the gash in the earth got done. In short,
he's the building, no matter where it goes.

I never am.
        No harm is done. A throb

lodges at the back of my eyes the day we start
and starts pulsing. Not a pain, and liquor makes
a dent in it. One gets so one can see
around it, and it stops the day we're through.
I'm just the same as ever. It's as if
I know I'm going to die before we reach
the roof. As if completing it required
the stilling of some unsatisfied critic,
and I am what it wants.

      It's morbid stuff,
but think: they never finish dead men's books,
and you don't pick up where Schubert left off,
but functionaries make themselves at home
when it's a building, and they freeze you out.
I should have been something else. Ideally,
something that doesn't die. Failing that, some
little man of property, with the one business:
make sons.

   In theory, architecture's
lovely. A man in space, actual as
the given world that shadows him, finally
up with the stars and mountains. Maybe. But
construction means delay in Boston Mass.
America is a hundred, and nothing works,
and I am cursed. To believe the beautiful
at all is bad for the nerves, but then to insist
that, as a star is a way of talking
about light, so beauty must be a glimpse
of a whole world—ah, that is like damnation,
Commodore.

    This church is not built upon
a rock, but you never know that for sure,
not on time. I came on the flaws by chance.
I took to climbing up the inner walls

because the ropes and catwalks went that way
and I was tired of pacing on the floor.
The painters rigged a floating studio
close to the roof. The gilder has a perch
that pulleys up and down. The ladders lean
so many ways you must give up on luck
and walk beneath a dozen at a time.
I am Trinity's monkey after dark.
Daredevil, breakneck, leaping through the night
like a wild idea. I guess I mean
to see if I got it right by brushing
every surface, meeting the lines of stress
eye to eye.
          What brought me to the window,
I don't know. The uppermost view, I think,
and a moment's fear of turning simian
for real. So stop, I thought, stop circusing,
and when I did, I eased out of the rafters
and clung, fully human again, to the hole
in my head, the highest highest window ledge—
eighty feet up, a circle cut like a moon
in the tower.
          What did I expect? Boston
does not aspire to be Nineveh and Rome.
It lay before me, lost to the dream of flight.
It wants to be close to the earth and so
be nearer death, taking its cue from life,
which five months of the year beds down with bones.
So there I was. I couldn't say how long.

I know what they want me to say, that I'm
so good I can't go on. Leaving to them
the walling up and the law whereby one lives
alone on narrow streets. Though I say "them,"

I don't, on the whole, mean people. Something there,
the muse's opposite, says "Don't sing." Some
creature of the air who wants us on the ground.
She tells me how I have learned the false fear,
of winter, to hide a nightmare: the better
art is, the more it comes to save itself
and changes nothing else.
                           I work in gray,
brown and black, the night-deep glimmer of rocks,
so I am being serious. Beauty
is not what I mean by what I would like
beautifully made. Things must be difficult
and cruelly austere. There has to be
a winter in the stone to stop the one
that palsies us. If they are hard and dark,
my buildings will survive this tiny age.
If they are lovely, they haven't a chance.
When I abandon this ruin to God,
I'm giving up heights, or I'll *say* I am
and go underground.
                        Look. More snow. I see
I've talked away the windless eye of the storm
and drained my cache of brandy. We'll go in.
I beg your pardon? Oh, I didn't know
you had so little time. Let me outline
your options—I can't put my hands on the plans,
but they're somewhere in this box. They'll turn up.
You could go the route of an obelisk—
they have an ancient air—or a wedding-cake
graveyard folly, which says you are gone on
but plan to keep your place. I don't deny
the civic glow attendant on a name
chiseled across a pediment, but it's
been done to death. We want so little style
the beautiful will lose its reason.

Blank

your mind, and lease to it a house afire
that the earth is restless to have returned.
When it burns, out in the winter woods, it has
the old raw sun on its mind, and form cannot
stand up to it. The error of our ways
is the wish for what lasts, based as it is
on the wreck. So make it better. Make it stone.
And why? What goes on is only the fire.

We'll go north. Or rather, our agents will.
On paper I have done an ice tower,
Gothic, totemic, at one with the spectered
city of snow where I want it soaring.
When they get there, the men can chip it out
of a glacier. Whatever works. But let them
make their compromises out of my sight.
For once I want to think the end as real
as all my visions of it. I've stood by
long enough.
          A lookout near the North Pole
will do it, but why not a further rule?
We'll write time in: "To be constructed when
the parties to this deal are dead." Trust me.
We require an impossible project.
Something ought to inhabit the region
beyond the reach of what we bring to pass.
I know too well what *I* do. I'm betting
the fully wintered year, the sleepless white
and the freeze of the sea, will wipe the roads away,
and I won't go. I believe I told you:
winter has stranded me, has starved me out
and asked me to recant. It has no room
for the man in the moon.
          Wait. Where are you off to?

I'm not joking, no, and yes, I'm sober.
Why? Are you backing out of our contract?
I'm not through. The new snow slows you down, see,
and besides, my voice carries to the far edge of
Trinity's plaza. You can't outrun it. Go
build an outhouse. I've been bellowing here
ever since the day I chalked the dead ground
commanding it to lift me up. You want
what they all want, the things I've finished with.
May the night wind take shelter in your name,
Commodore. May you lie down without stones.

Well, that's done that. And much more to the point
than saying no. You can come out now, White.
What do you want? Bourbon and branch? You know,
if he had had a go at the liquor-case
or the fire, either one, I'd have given in.
It's the last thing left to teach you: clients,
the care and feeding of. You gamble some.
You find you've thrown out half a year's business
over a drink—well, you may as well say
the brandy at least was up to snuff. Also,
it may be for a minute you were warm.
On balance, you don't do badly. Just don't
think you have to *build* them all. We are not
going to go to the sky because of tycoons.
Part of what we are is what we only
imagine we would do, were the time ours.
And we can live on that. To next year, then.
We'll do a castle truly in the air
and let it go. You'll see. We'll get there yet.

Musical Comedy

To César

Elyot: That orchestra seems to have a remarkably small repertoire.
Amanda: Strange how potent cheap music is.
        —Noel Coward, ***Private Lives***

May, 1935

I

> On the verge of Ohio
> (pray for me)

Cara—
        Well, nothing would have happened if
I hadn't had to pee. But I get bored
sleeping away the night, and getting up
gives me a breath of air. And just lately
I can't get back to sleep. I've always said
there ought to be trains for insomniacs,
special nightlies tooting to Liverpool
and back, with us rocking in little beds
like babies Mum has brandied the gums of.
Trains throw me in comas.
                        But not this trip.
I knew it at half-past three. I stood there,
my aim as shaky as a drunk sheriff's,
and thought, What if I have a heart attack,
I bet there's not a drop of digitalis
east of Chicago, once you've left New York.

87

And then, staring in the itsy mirror
above the sink, I couldn't imagine *what*
went on between Chicago and New York.
A kind of Salisbury Plain perhaps, without
the Druids. I hadn't a clue to the name.
I stood like a misled Genoan, pitched
at earth's edge, wondering where the curve went.
"Good God, man," I said, "see if there's a priest
on board. You want unction." I was rattling
the window down to duck my head out of—
seeking a kind of wind cure—when we stopped.

The night was like a cocktail, mixed and sweet
at the bottom, but there was nothing there
to speak of. Trees and all that, but no *place,*
no station. Goody, I thought, it's bandits.
Or a cow on the tracks. I leaned way out
and could see, because we were on a bend,
the whole of us, end to end, in an arc
like the curl of the new moon above us.
Everything had such—what do I mean?—shape,
I suppose. I'll never sleep again. Naps,
perhaps, but one owes the night an eye
made angry by the day's monotony
and not a lot of idiotic dreams.
Our nannies lied to us about the dark.
Fairies are people-headed after all
and spend a pot of money on their clothes
and wouldn't dance on the head of a pin
unless the press was asked.
                              What happened was
the thing they tell you not to put in books.
Out of nowhere, a woman in a veil

pearled by the moon appeared, crossing the plain
that seemed a moment since as desolate
as a thin remark of Arnold's. (Matthew
Arnold. Second-rate. A poet trapped in
the body of a boy scout.) I would swear
the moon had thought her up, except for this—
the closer she came to the train, the more
the sky was lit by lost planets so dim
and so far gone that I lost count. The moon
went out, used up in setting the tone. I saw
now, in her coming near, the proper scene
light up. The country depot and the man
who left her, one foot on the runningboard
of his cocoa Packard, his face hidden
in smoke from his cigar. I could have sworn
he was whistling a song I wrote—

> *A girl who had no elbows stole my heart.*
> *When we danced the tango we were very smart.*
> *But now that I've learned to make love at arm's length,*
> *Everyone's cheek to cheek.*

                          Just then the train
sent up its own soprano, cutting off
the songs the night could carry. She had reached
the tracks, and I had to bend from the waist
into the shivering country air (I don't
wear pajamas, they make me look like George
the Fifth's aunts, all of them), and she got on
and turned in the doorway and parted the veil
(but not so I saw), looking back at him.
They held the moment still between them. This,
I thought, is the way to go—it was clear

they were saying goodbye, that this was it,
and all without a word.
                         Then with a lurch
we went on, and I banged my poor head blue
pulling back in, like a turtle caught out
in a storm. I am a sucker for scenes
in which things done for keeps are given force
by people who have nothing left to lose.
They wear their lizard shoes to the crossroads,
and they get there early so they can pace,
or late and out of breath. Coincidence
is what they're giving up, and thus they plan
the final round down to the fingerbowls.
The things they do with a cigarette
are thicker than the fifth act of **Hamlet,**
and that's before they light it. It may be
love is cheap at making situations,
but what a vehicle for playing dead.

When you come right down to it, what I felt
was, *Christ,* I'm all alone. I didn't say,
but the men on this train—Raskolnikovs,
for the most part, who are beating it home
from college, pistols at their hips—are all,
as *my* aunt said about the *arrivés*
at the edges of her set: "N. O. S. D."
Not our sort, dear.
                     If I am to be chaste
coast to coast, I may type my way across.
Americans have never learned to write
anything in twenty minutes, but *I* have.
Backstage, in taxicabs, while cooling soups
in restaurants, I take a phrase to bits
or scribble scenes about mothers-in-law.

Once, standing in line at the bank, I did
a patriotic air. Which reminds me,
I promised you a thing or two to sing
last month. I will be humming it for you,
I promise, when you meet my train. It goes:

> *Where will I be in a year or two*
> *If I get so lost in a day or two*
> *With someone as bloody as you?*

That's as far as I've got. Will write again,
must sleep.

       Oh, in the end I put my head
out the *door* and said to the good captain—
"Where the hell are we?"

                      "Pennsylvania."
Calm as you please. I'm terrified.

                         Love, Noel.

II

Dear Marlene,
                    Whoever she is, she's
out of the Packard class. The porter says
the Pullman she's in is *hers,* with its own
liveried staff. It sounds like one of those
gunshy mountainous principalities
teeming with poppies, where the goats are gods.
She stays put. No name. The Madame X bit.
I'll bet my dad's insurance she's a spy,
clicking her infra-red, her ice eyes set,
plotting who knows what scheme for who knows whom.
I'm going in there unarmed. I owe it
to England.
                    Lunch. We will pull in
to Chicago this afternoon. Lilacs
are out in Europe, and they are more real
from where I sit than all this aimless green.
America's too big between the coasts,
so that the trees after a time lose sight
of what they are *vis à vis* the sea. Trees
are all they want to be. Salt is common
only at the table.
                    Which reminds me.
I am supposed to eat a fish that looks
as if a Japanese dried it in sand
to prop it among his pods, sauced with a froth
gone terribly gelatinous. My boiled
potato lies alongside, uninvolved,
like a bar of nice soap. My tablemate,
whom I would as likely have *chosen* as
I would a missionary with a rash
and an eye out for scraps, has told me twice
he is an Indian.
                    "What tribe??" I say.

He looks a bit phlegmy.
                "Fort Wayne," he says.
Can you picture how bleak *that* place must be,
an old cavalry post, the horses sore
and the souls whored. He certainly seems new
to the real world, or is eating his first
dinner on dishes.

          3 P.M. What comes
of being very bored is never nice,
as the police always say at the scenes
of posh suicides. "Mm," the inspector
remarks, sniffing the tooth glass, "It's like this,
they're sick of being boys, and dying seems
grown-up." It happened between the fish goo
and the heartbroken pudding. My Indian
fulminated. Remarks about his crops,
his tedious roadster, lumps in his lawn,
on his head, in his bed. I clucked and purred
and tried out rhymes in my mind to keep me
busy, when he confessed, "I had it up
before breakfast. I met this crazy girl,
and we did it."
            Did it? When did the tone
alter? I thought we were on to hay ricks
and fields of maize.
               "Don't get me wrong," he said.
"I'm a happily married man."
                    "How nice.
Where have you put her? A wife, don't you know,
belongs at a man's side." The squaws, they say,
make blankets all day long and brew green soups
in tents, I've seen it at the pictures. "Ah,
perhaps the ride on an empty stomach
has lain her low."
               "Eileen? I left her home.

The only thing *she* does in bed is sleep.
I mean a stranger. Nervous. Up all night.
I was having my juice—"
                              "Who is she?"
                                        "Who?
Some whore. She didn't take it off."
                                   "The veil?"
"They have diseases of the face sometimes.
I don't know. The body was okay. Thin.
She comes in in the middle of my juice,
I was the only one here, and she says—
'Where can I get a whiskey?'
                              'I don't know.'
'You want a whiskey?'
                         'Now? I want some eggs.'
'Eggs aren't going to get you anywhere,'
she says, laughing. Just as if it made sense.
Maybe because she's foreign. All the words
are there, but they don't work. Some women live
in different countries when they speak, with laws
that are only words."
                         "Shut up." And I stood,
wild-headed with the countries I had kinged
when she boarded, raving to be her knight,
but certain too that here the enemy
had the advantage of the deep summer
that lies on love's other side. I was here
on the near slope, spring, in the land of good
ideas. "I am a priest. Well may you
snivel and wish now you'd had the omelet,
but that, as the snake said, is applesauce.
People burn for less. Get out."
                                   "But Father"—
it seems he is an *Irish* Indian—

"I didn't know. You're dressed like—"

                                        The red queen's
jack-of-all-whatnot, he might have ventured,
but lacked the accent quite to bring it off.
I can't tell you how indescribable
I looked to him, ascot and suede trousers,
"Celia isn't this party crackerjack"
and all.

            "I'm in disguise," I said,
"doing a hush-hush job. The church today"—
I humphed like Bernard Shaw—"is politicked
and shady as a Baltic state. Anyone
might be—

            but I've talked too much. I must go.
Stay in your room."

                    I floated off, seeming
to faint with state secrets. And found her car
next the caboose. The butler at her door
proved firm, but when I said my name, she called
from deep inside to let me pass. I strode
through the beaded curtain into a moor's
pleasure-house, a sort of Persepolis
on wheels. It flashed through me that afterwards
I'd quiz my Indian why he left out
picturing the place. When there she was.

                                        "So you're
Dietrich's writer friend. She never mentioned
you were queer. Are you hungry? You want eggs?"

As easy as that. Festoons, and the floor
all pillows, a big brass table and the cats
on guard from an ivory zoo. And Garbo sat,
a bottle in her hands like Aladdin,
wishing the world away. A face no veil

could put out of focus, whose bones began
in Egypt, then swept west on the spring winds,
and in five thousand years were ready to
resolve themselves as this.

> "You have whiskey?"

"Sometimes," she said, "before I have breakfast.
Go find a glass."

> So I stood there thinking,
in this W. C. of a kitchen,
"I am getting a glass at Garbo's place,"
larking like an undergraduate. Oh,
the boy's smitten. All for now.

> Ravished, Noel.

This, P. S., is the doodle that I did
on my napkin. Pardon the fishy bits—

> *Oh don't come back, I've had it up to here*
> *With men whose hearts have vanished in a year.*
> *I'm all patched up and haven't shed a tear*
> *In twenty minutes. Oh don't remind me now.*
>
> *I'll be all right once you are on a yacht*
> *Outside the three-mile limit. I have bought*
> *A darling dog who loves me when I'm not*
> *So nice to be with. Oh don't remind me now.*

The end is meant to be breathy. La la
love is embers. Down in the throat. No tears.

III

We're just like—

    sisters, I almost said,
to tease you. Say roommates. In boarding school
over in Provence. Garbo would be the one
who knew, being from New York, how to wear
the hair, whatever the hour, and hitched her skirt
when walking in the hills. The nuns have draped
the mirrors, and the night is corridored
with the whir of bats, and still she pockets
ten quid a week smuggling cigarettes. Help,
sweet Kraut, let me not gush. I can count on
sirens and flags from you, Marlene dear,
who know a fool from a fitful writer
and why he tinkers at people's fences,
because he likes to overlook a field
pocked with hasty choices, wondering what
will grow.

    We are in Kansas. If you cut
all the grass, you would have the moon. The hills
agree with one another, and they have
no opinion, and no faith in latent
meaning. When we were drunk enough, we found
what was on our minds. I'd sworn off liquor
last month in New York, waking with a nail
driven in my head, having the night before
told my damp producer to mate his dogs
and his daughters. Garbo is something else.
One puts out the lights of resolutions—
nothing tighter than wine, keep pants buttoned,
eschew the parallels to Oscar Wilde—
and lurches round the dark like a lost moth
freed of the dance, mad to let a cottage
in a cardigan. It went like this—

      "Well,

I hear you write a lot of silly songs.
Do you ever get serious?"
                              "Never.
I do parlor tricks, even in my bath.
I wear a false nose, sometimes pendant from
my right ear. I sleep in the loo, dreaming
of jokes. Who was the man with the Packard?"

"Eric," she said, brushing it off like crumbs.
"You think you're second-rate, don't you? Someone
has to be Shakespeare. Don't you want to be?"

I do not like cushions, sitting as if
I had fallen on ice. I want my tea
at set hours. Dimly, I started to hurt
more than I thought her beautiful (like Keats,
the class item, all his boy's hair sweated
and flat against his head).
                              "Writing is best
kept in its place. It can't be spoken of.
Talk of Shakespeare is an impertinence
to writers. Makes them queasy. One must be
a tonic and potential man, unmarried to
the triple mistress—poems, dreaming, death—
by writing most off the top of one's head.
Eric who?"
                  "You're frightened. They'll laugh at you
if you try a *real* play. Give their tickets
to their servants."
                        "Unfair. It was your move."

This can't be what we said. I remember
we were funny, that we let it be known
we never slept and took to taking turns
at lullabyes.

Go to sleep, take a pill,
We are speeding after the sun, but shh,
We must let him win, the West is his,
And we are only going, going there.

Holding on like orphans of the storm, twined
on a divan in a seraglio, through
the new night, the second night out, Kansas
struggling out of the corners of our eyes
to make it known that sleep lies in the land
and not in our power. After a while,
whiskey washes down like the first hot kiss
of some new pleasure you're not ready for.

What are we going to do? An opera.
We have agreed to write it in one day,
to keep our thoughts in order, for outside
(I tell you this with something like the grief
I had thought was confined to books alone)
the *real* West has begun, prairie (*prairie,*
what a word), and everything seems very
angry and certain.
                              "I hate opera,"
she said, but I said it too. She said: "Why?
Because it takes too long. We'll make something
seriously broken into moments
when you might really sing and say something.
What kind of a name is Noel? English,
ambiguous. The name of a game of cards
or a woollen cape."
                              I must go. I do not,
I should add, say anything but Garbo
and thus haven't said yet what kind *she* is.
Of course I continue to love you.
                                        Noel.

IV

Utah, or perhaps Wyoming. *Somewhere.*

"When you're serious, what do you talk about?"
I asked.

"Beauty and time," she said, her arms
behind her head, in men's white pajamas,
the odalisque of the Union Pacific. "Keep love
out of it."

"No. You're just being bitchy."
(Eric *appears* to be a no-good boob
whose family's in steel. He dogs her now
and makes her ulcerish. She thought him dear
for about four hours.) "Love is quite profound
in the proper doses."

"You do the love songs.
I'll be the naturalist. I want music
an oak tree could whistle to an oak tree.
In fact, I don't want to do people much."

And that is how we began, like the two
Saturday mates, fuzzy in a pub. And one
says to the other, "How do I know I'm
really in love?" And the other one says, "Well,
you put some money down for a wedding ring.
That's real enough."

Well, we have just written
two-thirds of something real enough. Garbo,
I don't know why, says not to tell you yet,
but here I go. Keep it under your hat.

Brief synopsis of

The Boy in the West
by Noel Coward and Greta Garbo.

Beauty is trapped in the body of a boy
who lives on a leafed and wine-gold coast, muscled
and sunned, watched by his charmed companions three,
a porpoise, a hawk, and a bear, in whom poor Time
is held variously captive, in flux
among all three. The boy sings all day long
about the weather, he sings things *to* it,
boring his even-tempered friends. The hawk,
who tells him what is on the horizon,
sings a song about the cities waiting
to be built beneath them. The bear
keeps the boy in training, is his track coach,
and laments the age of heroes. Last, the gray
whistle-headed porpoise flutes the sun down—
he always has the *soul's* desire at heart.

In Act I, the boy greets the sun at length,
imagining anew the sea-edge seethe
and sea-fall. His design, what he has made
his own, is invisible, as if here
one slept in air, ate air heavy with wet
and honey, no misgivings and no waste.
He touches the place as delicately as
the constant sun in its day-to-day.
                       And then
the three creatures lecture. Blah-blah, sweetened
(as what isn't) by melody. Today
Time is the hawk, and He is going by.
But suddenly (finally) some sails are sighted.

(Every comedy is so like **The Tempest,**
it has to have a Miranda living a life
there, as well as an Ariel, who's queer.)
And they let off little boats that dimple
to the land of The Boy in the West, who sings,
"Come, there is so much room for us here."

                                    Horns.

Twenty or so Dickensian folk appear,
all criminals, a whole court plot against
a king, brought to exile. Flowers alone
they exempt from their hatred of outdoors.
They *loathe* country life. Bringing up the rear,
their warden, a pretty girl (unarmed), who sings,
"Notice the light. It is so *light* here, like
a dream."

            They catch sight of one another.

Act II.

The Bleakhouse Gang, onstage,
do a rousing number while they cut trees
and start their suburban villas. The boy,
having for love of her lost track of Time,
brings the girl back here to his harbor reach—
she has made him put on a woven cloth
over his privates (most fetching)—and sees
the hack work happening and moans.

                          "Stop them!"
he sings. "They will trust you."

                           "What's wrong?"
she wonders. "We are building a new world."
(In a comedy you write about being
happy, for which there are no images,
and the people in it disagree a lot.)

"Wrong!" rings out of the sky and up the beach
and then booms in the hills. Three lost voices
chorusing what's gone wrong. The hawk rides in
on the bear's brown shoulder, shrieking. Time itself,
he says, has brought this on, to ruin those
who hold Him to a form. No, says the bear,
for Time is over. They none of them hear
the clear kazoo of the porpoise, swimming off,
Time locked in his heart like a man in a boy,
trying to say that Beauty and Time will cease
to coexist. "Otherwise," he murmurs,
"nothing will change."
                              What can the poor girl do?
She's bound by law to civilize the place,
to make it St. Tropez. "We can't stop it,"
she sings, "but we will make it beautiful."
The Boy in the West, for love of her, agrees,
though Beauty, reading Proust in Her apartment
in his heart, can't abide the adjective
traded under Her name, and shuts Her book.

Once the boy yields, the wilderness latent
in everything comes true. The bear rumbles
and practices mauling. The hawk's good eye
turns to the dumb nut-gatherers who lunch
in the open. This is all done in a trio
in which the wordless fury that man can't
talk his way into is called back in—hawk
and bear and, faintly, the beep and toot from the sea
where the porpoise has tried to flee with Time.
"Growl" goes the world. Time is no longer held,
not one thing and not another. The boy,
for love of her, is deaf. The curtain falls.

When I am with her, Marlene, I feel
like Nora running away with Hedda.
I feel like I am coming to summer.
Of all the passages that I have made,
I have not won this one. Ironic, that.
I am the great writer of shipboard romance.
I will be in L.A. at nine thirty
tomorrow, in the A.M.

Ta ta, Noel.

V

Lili M.—

  I am writing a fifth time
to separate what's gone from what's gone on.
No time to post it. There isn't a place
between here and there. I'll hand it to you,
you can read it later. You won't like it.

It started with (everything does, in a way),
"Let's go to bed."

      "But we won't sleep," I said,
dead at the piano. We had written
two acts in fourteen hours, right on schedule,
and said let's break to catch our breath. Outside,
a desert warred with a stack of mountains.

          "No,
I mean let's fuck."

      "Don't be perverse. I don't
go with ladies."

      "So what? Sometimes I drop
an egg in a whiskey, raw. It doesn't mean
I've given up ice. Is it very small?"

"What? My thing? It depends. Don't be lurid.
Or intimate. You won't budge a button."

"I thought we were getting serious."

          "Did you?
It is a word you use far too often,
the way an Eskimo might say 'fish.' We are
getting our sea legs. Getting West. *I* thought
we were after loftier things than us."

The line of that mouth. Like a line on a map

drawn from Caesar's to Cleopatra's city,
the distance between two points, just as Shaw saw,
but with the added weight of the going there.
One knows what Garbo means before she speaks.

"I want to be alone for a while. You're right
about one thing. I know my way around
a ship. I'm built like Popeye. Do you mind?"

"No no," I said. "I'll get my things together."
(I'd not been in my room since Illinois.)
"There ought to be a proper interval
before Act III, so we can pee and fix
our faces. Ta."

        Speedy exit. Foxtrot
from car to car, the homeless boy, coursing
the badlands under someone else's steam,
no stops. What is it the knight feels, riding,
when he can no longer make out the scarves
billowing from her tower? That he must
keep the tower now for his destiny,
his life a circle meant to bring him back.
The queen can be The Beginning till he moves.
The least movement changes her into The End.
That is how quests are undergone.

        In my room,
of all people, the Indian lay fast
asleep. Well well. His sheep eyes popped open,
and he went into the Emily Post routine
Americans are dreariest at. "Gee whiz,
Father, I must have fallen off." Brilliant.
"I feel so bad, I've mussed your bed."

             "Tell me,
what are you here for?"

          "I want to confess."

The ensuing scene, the deleted scene, is pure
pornography. Cut. Not because you can't
take the facts. More because we must be free,
as I pull in, of the diversions of
the *entr'acte.* Likewise, facts are not comic
or musical, and one bit of singing
remains to sound, thin as the porpoise's kiss.
I mention the Indian at all to prove
everyone sleeps in the end with everyone else,
though not onstage. He proves our pain is not
carnal. Garbo and I were both *satisfied,*
as far as that goes.

              How long does it take
to bring these things to a head? Perhaps an hour.
Two at most. It's true, we dozed off. I woke.
It was dark. I left him and all my things
and sprinted east. Oh wait.

                  She was waiting,
veiled, outside our Aladdin's car. She seemed,
in the no-man's-land between two coaches, lost
to us and our faith in places. She'd flung wide
the door, and the night rushed us, longing to fan
her face.

       "Good. I wasn't going to wait,"
she said, "but now you'll know. I finished it.
The bear kills the girl. The boy kills the bear.
The hawk plummets, aiming right for his eyes.
The boy as he's blinded cracks the hawk's wings.
All of their ghosts sing at the end."

                      "I see.
and the porpoise?"

             "Drowns. He doesn't sing a note
in Act III. Too upset. Excuse me."

Then
she reached behind my head and yanked a cord,
and bells rang and lights flashed. We slowed and slowed.

"What did you do that for?"
                    "I have to go."

And so we stopped. I don't know where we were.
We were in clouds, no a fog but wet, drenched
with the air that clings around mountains.
                              "Really,
don't leave, I mean I don't care what we are,
but dammit—"
              "This has nothing to do with *you*.
It's that Eric expects me in L. A.
done up like a slave girl. This is his train,
you know. It's his whole damn *railroad* we're on.
He buys silly people by the carload. You see,
you have to be serious just to breathe.
Goodbye. We'll meet again. The same people
are after us both."
                Ah but don't you see,
what if they get me first? I'm going west,
and I can't keep it straight which way is up.
I'll be awake, the stars will be about,
and the strange, traveling lover that rides in me
will never come back. Forgive me. I've come
to think some places are the songs we sing.

"Where is *The Boy in the West*?"
                              "I threw it out."
"It's half mine. I want it."
                        "I threw it out
the *window*. The wind took it. You don't need it."

109

The train jerked and began, and she leapt down.
Oh I am an oak whistling after an oak.
I leaned out, and the train blew the veil up
just enough for the full moon in her eyes
to pass from cloud to cloud. And we held still,
though The Wild West Show rolled on, this way and that.

John Donne, our great comic actor, has a prayer
written on a horse—I mean, while he was
riding. And he's traveling west because
he can't bear his muse (in his case it's God),
because it makes him laugh when he would cry
about Beauty, and how It just goes out.
I have been alone about two hours now,
so I will be all right if there's the press
wanting to know who my characters are
in *real* life, as if there could *be* real life
as time-bound as a play. In just two hours,
you can watch Prospero go back to town.

At least I have got the right thing for you.
Here is a serious song I wrote today,
the love left out of it. I'm not afraid
of L.A. the way I am of New York.
Here, I know, a spade is a spade and not
a heart. Sing this for what in us is still
lost in transit.

Home on the Southport Car.

My father came home on the Southport car,
A kind of club for commuting men.
It took them home to Connecticut
And back each day to New York again.

He wasn't much more than a banker then,
Not as rich as a man in stocks,
But he showed a great flair for backgammon
On the Southport car, where there are no clocks.

A lovely man. And I had a horse,
And my mother a mink that was a miracle.
On Friday nights they went out to dine.
And he did get a raise. That's empirical.

So why fall in love on the Southport car,
When you can do it at the Plaza?
Once you have read your Henry James,
You want to know first where the bars are.

But he fell in love with a journalist
Whose pieces appear in the New York World,
A man of alarming ancestry,
An Irishman, his hair all curled.

Now they are both intellectuals,
And they have a place on the coast near Rome,
And the Southport car goes back and forth,
But it does not bring my father home.